I press my lips together as I
"Twenty-two. But in my defens
Twenty-two is Lucas's number,"
such good friends.

Shea doesn't miss a beat. "A
have stayed in a six-room cabin th
Elli. Did you pay for all those lights to be put up too?"

Yes, I did. "No," I fib, and he rolls his eyes as he lifts our suit-
cases out of the snow. Shea stands bigger than ever, with a little
more weight around his hips than he cares for. For me, I love it.
Being a hockey player for so long, he was always so trim. But that
was Shea Adler, defensive powerhouse for the Nashville Assassins.

Oh, how I love that man. We've built one hell of a life, had five
gorgeous, talented children, and somehow survived all of them,
mostly unscathed. Shea Adler as a dad is a sight that can't be
unseen. He loves his kids and puts his whole self into them. Each
one knows their daddy loves them and that he would honestly lay
down his life for them. He taught them to be patient, to be kind,
but most of all, to love. He showed our girls how to be loved by a
man, and our boys how to love a woman.

All by loving me.

It all seems like time has gone so quickly, but the years show on
his handsome face. The wrinkles around his eyes, the gray in his
beard and on the sides of his head. My PopPop, as our eldest
grandson Zac calls him. I really don't know how I've been lucky
enough to fall for Shea repeatedly all these years, but now that he's
a grandpa, I wish like hell that I could freeze time and just stand in
awe of him. Crazy as it sounds, I think Shea as a grandpa may be
my favorite. He loves our grandbabies like he loves their mommas.
With his whole body and soul.

I'm not one to question if my husband loves me; I know he
does. But he's staring at me, one brow cocked and his lips pursed.
"You're lying."

I shrug innocently. "Fibbing."

Shea shakes his head as he walks in my direction. "This is ridiculous. So over the top. And just know, when my parents, and Lucas, Fallon, Grace, and whoever else shows up and teases you for going overboard, I won't defend you."

I hold back my laughter. He will. I know he will. I look up at the massively huge chalet that will hold my whole family for the holidays, a little worried I did go overboard. Yes, it's rather large. And yes, it's covered basement to roof with Christmas lights. And yes, maybe there is an inflatable Grinch scene. Oh, and a life-size nativity. But I couldn't help myself. "I just love Christmas!"

"Elli," is all he says as he comes toward me. He drops one bag in the snow and points to the door. "Tell me now. Is the inside just as bad?"

I bat my lashes at him. "Define bad."

His eyes burn into mine, and he knows that inside could be the film set for any Hallmark movie. "How many Christmas trees?"

I press my lips together. "Like, a total? Or small trees and then floor-to-ceiling trees?"

He lets his head fall back, closing his eyes as he groans my name. "Eleanor. Am I sleeping in a Christmas sleigh?"

I smile widely at him, wrinkling my nose as he looks back down at me. "No, but there is a lot of mistletoe in our room."

Annoyance leaves his face almost instantly as he gazes into my eyes. He reaches out, taking my jaw in his large, callused hand. I smile as he grins down at me, his dimples taking my breath away. He strokes his thumb along my lips and leans down to kiss me. Before he does, he says, "How many trees?"

"One in each room, and if they didn't fit, then I did small trees."

He closes his eyes, resting his nose on mine. "You drive me insane, woman. Utterly insane."

My grin widens. "I know you love me."

"More than you'll ever know."

He kisses me then, and I cuddle deep into his chest. Not only

A Smoky Mountain Hockey Holiday

NASHVILLE ASSASSINS : NEXT GENERATION

TONI ALEO

Editing: Silently Correcting Your Grammar: Lisa Hollett - AS ALWAYS, THANK YOU!

Proofer: Jenny RaRden - THANK YOU!

Cover: Care Dee - THANK YOU!

❀ Created with Vellum

To myself:
You made it. You did it, and you didn't give up.
Good job

A Smoky Mountain Hockey Holiday

By Toni Aleo

Surprise!

Elli Adler

As the truck door slams, I look back at my husband's very confused face and smile brightly. I glance over at the chalet I rented for the Christmas holiday, and I am just so giddy with excitement, I'm shaking.

All my kids, all my family, and all my grandbabies under one roof. I'm squealing internally!

"Eleanor Adler. What the hell?"

I grin at him, throwing up my hands in enthusiasm. "Surprise!"

Shea glares. "Elli, you said we were getting a cabin."

"No—a chalet," I correct. He doesn't appear to have the patience for my extravagance.

"This is a mansion," he states matter-of-factly as he watches me in disbelief.

"No. It's a chalet, and we have potentially twenty people who are going to be here for the holidays. We needed space."

"Yes, like six rooms. This is what, twenty?"

for the closeness but for the warmth. It's cold as hell in the Smokies, but I knew it'd be the perfect place for everyone to meet up. With the boys in South Carolina, I wanted to make the trip easy for them. I knew that everyone from Nashville would have to drive, but I wanted a real white Christmas. Of course the Smokies have delivered. The mountaintops are covered with beautiful blankets of snow, and so is the chalet. It's moody and magical as darkness approaches, but for me, it's perfect. Most everyone will be here by morning except Evan and his girlfriend Callie since they're doing Christmas Eve morning with Callie's family. I extended the invite to them, but Evan didn't seem to want to extend it further.

I was under the impression that everything was fine with Callie's sister and her husband, but maybe something happened. I don't know, and I honestly don't care, because Evan is so happy. The change from being broken and lost because he retired early from the NHL into the man he is now still brings me to tears. I'm just so proud, and oh, I can't wait to see him and Callie. She is so good for my boy, and I adore her sweet face.

When the crunching of snow disrupts our kiss, we both turn to see our billet son, Benson, pulling in beside our truck, with our youngest son in the passenger seat. My babies. When we opened our home to Benson, I wasn't aware how much I would love him. He is such a sweet boy, and being able to be here for him as he navigates college is a blessing. He had a chance to go to the juniors, but he chose to go to school instead. The University of Bellevue is one of the top hockey colleges in the US, so he knew he would still have a chance to draft. Benson waves as he parks, but my heart is heavy for him.

He's had a rough couple of months, and I know he isn't over what happened at the end of his freshman year. I think that's why he isn't going home for the holidays—not only because he doesn't want to stop training, but because he doesn't want to tell his mom that he'd gotten a girl pregnant and she chose to terminate the pregnancy. I am extremely proud of the way he supported and stood beside her through the whole thing. I've heard they don't talk anymore, but I know he knows that he did right by her.

Shea kisses my nose as the boys hop out. I wave to them while Shea goes to help with the endless amounts of gifts we brought. We had to drive two trucks to bring all the presents. With it being Fitzgerald's first real Christmas since he was too little to do more than sleep on his actual first Christmas, I am excited...and may have overbought. Hope Aiden and Shelli have room in their car to take everything back with them.

"Hey, guys!" I call as both boys look up at the chalet.

My baby, Quinn, looks back at me, blue eyes like his daddy's and looking every bit like his dad did when I met him. "I really don't think you got a big enough place for us."

"Har-har," I throw back, and he laughs, which brings a wide grin to my face. Quinn is in his first year of residency, and we are so astonished by him. We always thought he was extremely advanced when he was younger, but we really didn't think we could have made a genius. We did, and it's Quinn. The older kids always get upset, and they say that we saved all the smarts for Quinn. It's not true; all our kids are successful. Quinn is just...something entirely different.

"Over forty trees inside," Shea says, and Quinn gawks at me.

"So that's the real reason you rented this, so you can have more trees," he accuses, and I laugh.

Benson chuckles. "I don't know... She makes those trees fit. She put a tree on the back of my toilet. It's decorated with toilet paper."

Quinn and Shea shake their heads as I smile proudly. "I even made little rolls of toilet paper to hang like ornaments."

I swear I hear one of them call me crazy, but before I can complain, we are hurrying inside with all gifts. In the middle of the great room, beside a large stone fireplace where a stocking is hung for everyone, is a gorgeous floor-to-ceiling spruce that could give Joanna Gaines a run for her money. I had come up with Grace at the beginning of the week and put all our family ornaments on the tree for all the families coming. I wanted it to look like we took everyone's individual trees and made one huge one. Grace called me crazy, but I didn't care. It came out perfectly. The décor of the home is very rustic and woodsy. Everything is decorated for Christmas, but there is also a bear theme throughout the house. When I see a large taxidermied bear in the corner by the kitchen, tears gather in my eyes. "Aw, Shea, remember when I took the kids to Bass Pro Shop that one Christmas to get Karson and Lacey that gift card?"

Shea looks up, and when he sees what I'm standing beside, he laughs loudly. "Oh, when Quinn pulled on the bear's dick?"

Quinn snorts as Benson looks horrified. "What?"

"While holding his own penis," I add. "And yelling, 'Look, Ma, the bear has a dick like me!'" I exclaim, and Benson falls over laughing as Quinn nods arrogantly.

"Even back then, I was hung like a bear," he says proudly. "You should have taken a picture."

I shake my head as the door opens, and Shea's twin, Grace, enters the chalet with bags in her hands. "Quinny, Benson, go get the rest of the bags, please."

The boys agree and head out as Shea goes to help her. "I got everything on the list, and I hope you're ready to start cooking for all these damn people. We should have catered."

I glare at her. "I'm not taking someone from their family on the holidays."

"No, you'll just work your sister-in-law into the ground."

We hug tightly before we start to unload all the goodies she has gotten for us. Grace is distracted as she directs the boys and Shea, though I know she'll never admit it. Ever since we lost James, she hasn't been the same. Her eyes aren't bright anymore, nor is there any joy in her smiles. She misses him, especially around the holidays. I know in my heart, though, that with Ryan, his wife, and

Amelia and her family coming, it should provide some happiness for her. I hope it does, at least.

Shea and the boys go back outside to get the rest of the bags, and I lean into her. "How was your date?"

She rolls her eyes in true dramatic fashion. "Awful. Men are dumb. He just assumed I would sleep with him."

"Ew." Honestly, you couldn't pay me to date nowadays.

"Exactly. It was pathetic, and I hated it. So, I acted like I had the shits and left. Went home, got drunk, and got off with my Edward Cullen dildo." She winks at me. "Thanks. I love that thing."

I look at her, confused. "I bought that like ten years ago. It's still working?"

She nods. "Hey, he's a vampire. They live forever and sparkle while doing it."

Speechless, I shake my head as she snickers beside me. "It'd be nice to get some real dick, don't you think?"

"Yes. But unless it's attached to a nice guy, I don't want it."

She's right, but man, I hate seeing her sad. "True."

I move around her to wash the produce just as my phone rings. To my surprise, it's my best friend's sister Piper. "Piper! Hey!"

"Hey, sis. How are you? Merry Christmas!"

We fall into easy conversation, and it excites me to hear from her. She and her family moved to Russia maybe eight years ago, and their eldest, Dimitri, has blown up there in the KHL. He has a killer shot, and we love watching him play. I wish he played for my team, the Nashville Assassins, but he chose the KHL instead.

"So, the reason I'm calling is, we're coming home."

My lips curve up. "No way! Really?"

"Yeah, we plan to move back after Katarina is done with school this summer."

"Isn't it only her junior year?"

"Yes, but Dimitri wants to play for the Assassins. He isn't happy in the KHL anymore."

Surprised by that, I listen, and I am over the moon with eagerness. Shea walks in and makes a face as he listens to my side of the conversation. When we hang up, he looks over at me. "Who was that?"

"Piper Titov. They're coming home, and Dimitri wants to play for the Assassins."

Shea raises his brows, and then he shakes his head. "Good luck with that. Shelli is going to fight you on it."

I wave him off. "I haven't retired from my role as owner yet, and I always told Dimitri he'd be welcome on our team."

"Yes, but he chose the KHL, not us, and Shelli will hold that against him."

"You'll see. It'll all work out. We're all family."

"Yeah, but Shelli's hockey team isn't about family ties, Mom. It's about winning," Quinn says, and Benson points to me.

"She told me if I didn't clean up my skating, she wouldn't even let me in training camp."

I roll my eyes as Shea agrees. "I mean, you do need to be faster."

Benson nods. "I know."

"I'm not worried. Shelli will support my request, and everything will be just fine. It's Christmas. Look around... It's intoxicating in here!"

"I need to be intoxicated so I don't puke from the Christmas overload," Grace teases, and Shea nods.

"Wine?"

"Is that a question? 'Cause the answer is always yes." Grace grins widely as her twin gets up to pour her a glass. I ignore them both and check my phone to see where Shelli is. They haven't even gotten to Knoxville yet, so I have time to come up with a good reason for why we need Dimitri Titov. Not only is he a good player, but his dad played with Shea for years. We have spent many of our family gatherings with them. Shelli and Dimitri used to be close. Surely she'll be supportive and not fight me on it.

Or maybe I'll wait, because as I look around at the beautiful

Christmas splendor that is our home for the next few days, I don't want anything to ruin this. Unfortunately, as Quinn said, Shelli is focused on winning. It's her only focus, and I know she is already working on her plan for the summer, the draft, and training camp. I'll just need to figure out how to include Dimitri in those plans.

And not have it ruin our incredible Smoky Christmas.

You Put a Baby in a Box?

Fallon

"The mountains are always so pretty in the snow."

I feel my husband's gaze on me, and when I look at him, he's smiling. "Not as pretty as you."

I grin, but our youngest, Emery, gags loudly. "Aren't y'all done being all lovey-dovey? Doesn't that die out as the years go on? Like, how long have you two been together? A hundred years? Yes, Dad, we all know you get a boner for Mom. Ugh."

I press my lips together to keep from laughing as Lucas looks in the mirror at her. "You've been a joy these last six months. Truly, a joy."

Oh, the sarcasm is real. In all honesty, Emery has been more of a terror than usual. We don't know what happened, and we really don't understand what is going on. To us, Emery is thriving. She is studying criminal justice at Bellevue, and she sold her concept for some kind of camera that cops can wear. Pretty sure the kid is worth more than us. She is also working part time with the FBI Cyber Division and is included in all the development of said camera thing. I still don't understand it, nor do I care too much. I just want my baby to be happy.

And move out.

It'd be really great if she could move out.

I never in a million years thought it would be Emery who wouldn't leave. I swore, the moment she turned eighteen, she'd be gone. But she doesn't want to leave. *Has no reason to.*

There is a reason—I want to have loud sex with my husband.

And drink wine unjudged.

I have to remind myself daily that I love this child. I do, just as I love all my kids. Aiden is doing Aiden things, growing a family, and kicking ass on the ice. While Shelli can be a lot, she is everything that Aiden needs, and so I love her. Even when she gets on my ever-loving nerves. Shea and Elli did no one any favors by spoiling that girl rotten.

Though, I may have done the same with Emery...

I never really thought Stella would settle down, but she has. She is the full-time manager of our family restaurant and does the morning shift with Audrey at the cupcakery. She's opening two more restaurant locations across Nashville and planning a rather small wedding to her boo, Wes. Oh, I love that guy. He loves my daughter in a way that reminds me of Lucas's love for me. It's sweet.

I thought it'd be Asher who wouldn't move out, ever, but he proved me wrong. Hell, we hardly see the kid and Ally anymore. Thank God for FaceTime. They are traveling all over for Asher to work on jumbotrons across the US. We haven't seen him in over six months, which is why this trip is so special. Everyone will be together. I'll get to hug my baby, make sure he is healthy, and love on my daughter-in-law. Sometimes I worry that she thinks I don't like her, but I do, a lot. She and Asher just aren't around for me to prove that.

At her daddy's statement, Emery groans, "Whatever."

"You know, baby girl, we want a love like ours for you," Lucas says, and I shake my head. He's chancing his life, stepping into her lion's den.

"Y'all's 'love' is not real anymore, Dad. It doesn't happen that way. This world is full of bullshit and shit-ass guys. Then when you come across a decent guy, they just expect you to give yourself to them, and who wants to do that?"

"I did."

"Me too," I say after Lucas. "It's nice to be loved."

"Sure, but I don't want to be suffocated. I want to live. I want to have fun. I just don't want to deal with the bullshit."

"Are you okay, Em?" I ask, even though I know she won't answer me.

"Fine," she says, angrily throwing down her phone. "I hate people, and I don't want to go to this stupid family Christmas."

"Emery, you love the family, and you'll get to see Fitzgerald and Zac. You love the kids," I offer, but she doesn't seem to be into the idea of playing with babies. She really is on another level today. "Plus, you get to see Asher and Ally. I know you miss them."

"Yes, more displays of happy couples. Just what I want."

Lucas glances at me, and I shrug. He then looks in the mirror at her. "Wow, lots of feelings. Did you take your meds today?" Lucas asks, and Emery groans.

"No. I packed them before I took them, and I don't feel like getting them."

"Do you want me to stop?"

I press my lips together to keep from laughing as I smack his thigh.

Around his laughter, he says, "I can help you find them."

"Oh my God, Dad, you are so funny," she calls to him, and then she disappears under her blanket. I look at Lucas as he looks back, and we both shake our heads. No one prepares you for the transition from teenager to young adult. With the first three, it seemed a lot easier. But with Emery, it's a struggle. She doesn't talk to us or tell us what's going on. It took a family dinner for us to know she was sleeping with Quinn Adler.

Oh. My. God.

"Are you in a bad mood 'cause you have to see Quinn?"

As soon as the words leave my mouth, I regret them. From under the covers, she growls, "Quinn Adler has no control over my emotions, and I will not dignify that question with an answer."

"You kinda did," Lucas pokes, and I smack him again. "I really don't know why you'd be upset over him. You are the one who ghosted him."

We found that out from Stella. "I hate my sister."

"Emery, it's been six months. I'm sure it won't be awkward." She grumbles something, and Lucas laughs. Calmly, I add, "Or maybe he's still into you, and you get a second chance?"

"There wasn't even a first chance, Mom. We had sex. We were best friends, he ruined that, I ghosted him, let it die," she growls, and Lucas looks at me, wide-eyed. I know he's asking me how Quinn ruined it, and I sure as hell don't know.

"Do I need to kick his ass?"

"Oh my God, let it go!" she begs, and I press my hand to his thigh. Then she says, "Stella and Wes are there and wondering when we will be there."

I glance at the GPS as Lucas says, "Six minutes."

And we ride on in silence, both of us concerned for our daughter—and now our holiday.

Because Emery Brooks upset means no one will have a good time.

* * *

"Good God, Elli, you outdid yourself," I gush over my longtime friend as I take in the gorgeousness of our chalet. Elli smiles proudly at me. I just adore her. She has such a huge heart and loves making things special for everyone. Elli has always been like that. I have watched her care for her hockey team like she does her kids. She goes out of her way to make everyone feel like they're at home. When players haven't been able to afford to go home for the holidays, she sends them. She has given housing to the players, and her philanthropy is out of this world. She is a great mother, a great grandmother, a great wife, and makes all of us look bad. You can't hate her, though; you can only love her.

"Thanks. I am so happy and so excited. A bit gassy from the nerves, but I am so excited to have everyone under the same roof."

I laugh as Emery comes in with her blanket over her head, only showing her eyes. Elli turns to her and, to my surprise, gets a wide smile from Emery. "There is my sweet girl. How are you? How's the development of EMQUINNY coming along?"

The way she says that makes me feel like Emery named it after her and Quinn, but surely that's not the case.

Emery nods as she says, "Real good. We're working on the tech side right now, but it should start rolling out to Nashville Metro and some surrounding precincts starting in May. I got an email on the way up that California and Arizona are wanting to be a part of the trial, but of course I'm doubting myself and thinking it's not a good idea to go that wide yet."

I shrug. "Sometimes the risk is worth the reward. If they know there might be bugs and they can be patient, what's it going to hurt?"

She stares at me with a deadpan expression. "There will be no bugs. The only thing that can go wrong is user error, which stresses me out because people can be so damn dumb," she complains and then looks to Elli. "I'm hungry, and as my dad so kindly put it, I need my meds."

Elli smiles, tapping Emery's cheek. "Food is out on the counter, and drinks are in the fridge."

Emery turns and leaves as Elli looks at me.

I roll my eyes. "She's in a mood."

She chuckles. "I can tell. I'd say let Quinn take care of it, but he told me Emery isn't returning any communication."

"I heard the same. Any reason why?"

Elli shakes her head. "Girl, I asked, and he got defensive and walked away. I don't have time for it. They'll figure it out."

"Agreed," I say. Then I decide to ask what she thinks. "Do you think EMQUINNY is named after the both of them?"

She stops. "Well, hell. It sure does sound like it is. Could that be why they are having issues?"

"I honestly don't know," I say, a little sick over it. "I'll ask the boys when they get here."

"I'll ask Stella."

Just then, before either of us can go asking anyone, the door flies open and Asher comes in, carrying a huge box. My heart sings as he gently sets it down, and I go right for him. He meets me halfway, hugging me tightly as tears gather in my eyes. I squeeze him and take in his scent. Woodsy with a bit of spice. It's the cologne I got for him for Christmas last year. "Oh, Asher, I've missed you."

He squeezes me. "I missed you too, Mom."

I pull back as he does and take in all his features. He's gained a little weight, but it suits him. His eyes are bright and his nose red. You can tell he's happy. I look at Ally as she comes to me, hugging her too. "Oh, I've missed you! How are you?" I gush, and she hugs me tightly.

"Good. Excited to see you," she says, hugging me again. "Is my mom here?"

On cue, Harper scoops up her daughter, kissing her loudly on the cheek and starting to cry. I wrap my arm around Asher as Lucas comes in for a big, burly hug, basically hugging us both. I watch as Jakob hugs and kisses his daughter, and then both Titovs greet Asher. I am so thankful for how they've accepted my son and love him. All of us being together and raising our kids, it seems only normal that they would. But of course, as a mother, you worry for your child.

"So, we got an early Christmas gift for you guys," Asher says, and then he carefully picks up the nicely wrapped gift and sets it on the table. "Not everyone—just Mom, Dad, Harper, and Jakob. Though everyone will enjoy the present."

Ally grins widely, going to her husband and cuddling into his side. I can't believe they ended up together. I'd wished for it since Ally is wonderful, but they always seemed to keep things on a friend level. Oh, how grateful I am. They are so in love. He looks down at his wife and kisses her nose. "You ready?"

She nods eagerly and then walks over to unlock the side of the box. I didn't even realize it opened like that, but then, none of that matters. As the panel opens, I am confused by what I'm seeing. Harper gasps, and Jakob seems confused. I look at Lucas as he gawks at both Ally and Asher. I just stand there like an idiot, unsure of what I am looking at.

Asher lifts a bucket car seat from the box and brings it out, showing all of us a little bundle of pink. Instantly, I know that's Asher's baby. She has his nose.

"Oh my God," I gasp, and Lucas starts to laugh.

"You put a baby in a box!"

"Whose baby is it!" Harper yells.

"Is it yours?" Lucas asks, and I am speechless.

Asher and Ally look back at us proudly. "Surprise! We'd love to introduce you guys to your granddaughter, Alexis Fallon Harper Brooks," Ally says, her eyes bright and gorgeous.

And then, it's complete mayhem. Everyone freaks out, congratulating them and trying to get details. Also, trying to get to the baby.

"When?" Lucas asks.

"Three weeks ago," Asher answers. "We wanted to surprise everyone, so we kept it a secret."

"It wasn't easy," Ally said happily. "And you don't know how many times I wanted to call and ask for some kind of guidance, but we knew we wanted to surprise y'all."

I am utterly dumbfounded as I gaze down at my beautiful granddaughter. I stroke my finger along her cheek, and I'm completely in love. "She's perfect."

"She is," Lucas agrees as we stare down at her.

"Please tell me you're not traveling anymore," Harper says, and Asher nods.

"I'm strictly going to work for the Assassins and surrounding rinks."

Ally adds, "We want to make sure that Alexis has her family around her."

Tears run down my face as I kiss this sweet baby on her nose. She moves a little but not enough to wake up. I look at my son, and the pride I feel is overwhelming. I want to be mad they hid this, but am I surprised? No. They hid their love for each other, hid their marriage, and now a baby. They're private, and I can appreciate that. Both grew up with pro hockey-playing dads, so I can get why they'd want to keep things for themselves. Plus, I can't help but be proud they did it on their own and wanted to surprise us. I move my gaze back to my granddaughter Alexis and my heart soars.

It's overwhelmingly insane how quickly time passes. But boy, what a ride.

She Is My World

Aiden

I check the mirror to make sure Fitz is sleeping soundly as Shelli types violently into her phone beside me. A new renovation of the Nashville Assassins' housing is starting after the new year, and Shelli is overseeing the progress. I wish she wouldn't take on so much, but she's her mother's child. She's a workaholic. She loves to be in the middle of everything and show she is worth it all, but I wish she'd slow down. I'd like to knock her up again sooner rather than later. But every time I bring up trying for a second child, she wants to remind me how busy she is.

It's annoying as fuck.

When she sets down her phone and groans loudly, I ask, "Everything okay?"

"I am over this contractor. He's claiming that he doesn't want to do it my way, where they do the housing in sections. He wants to gut everything at once and renovate, but I still have six guys living there. So, I offered to have them share, and then he can do the first eight and finish the last three this summer. But he's pushing back. He's now saying he'll only do two at a time, which will take a year. I am so annoyed."

I bring my brows together, scrunching my nose. "But he knew people were living there. And didn't he say he could do it in sections when you hired him?"

"Yes, hence my annoyance. I am sending out letters to my other contacts to see if anyone is available. I want this done before training camp so everyone has a place to stay."

The guys who are staying in housing now are only there because they're having houses built. "You know, a lot of the other guys would open up rooms in their houses if we needed to get the ones in housing out so the construction company can just gut and go."

She nods. "That's an idea. I don't know. Let me see what I hear back. I wish he would just do it the way we discussed."

"That would be easier."

"For sure," she says, rolling her eyes and glancing back down at her phone. "Oh, Ally made an Instagram post. That's odd... Oh my God! Aiden! They had a baby!"

I almost wreck the car at the news. I look at where she's holding out her phone, to see my brother and his wife holding a bundle of pink. "What the hell? What does the caption say?"

I can hear the excitement and shock in Shelli's voice as she reads, "'The cat's out of the bag. We had a baby! Introducing Alexis Fallon Harper Brooks.' Aww! Born on December first. Did you know?"

"No! That jackass," I say in disbelief. "I talk to that dude daily, and he never told me." I reach for my phone, calling my brother. I feel Shelli's gaze as he says hello, but I don't greet him the way he did me. "I had to find out on Instagram that I'm an uncle?"

Asher chuckles. "You were supposed to be here when we got here, and as always, you're late. Also, aren't you driving? Why are you on your phone?"

"Shelli isn't driving!" I protest. "What the hell? How did you keep this from everyone?"

"We knew we wouldn't see anyone for the whole pregnancy, so we figured we'd just surprise everyone."

He's so private; it's weird. I'm his fucking brother, and he didn't even tell me. "Wow, I am shocked."

"Shocked you're an uncle, or shocked I didn't tell you?"

"Both, jackass."

He laughs. "Promise, no one knew. But I am sorry you had to find out on Instagram. I just realized Ally posted that."

"Okay, so I should yell at her?"

"You can try, but I'll take you out."

I scoff as he laughs. "Fine. Congratulations, asshole."

"Thanks. We're really happy, and she's beautiful."

"Shit, only if she looks like Ally," I tease, and he laughs.

"Nope. Spitting image of me."

"Gross," I say, but his laughter is intoxicating. "I guess Stella's next."

"Please. It'll be Emery before her. Stella won't even set a date with Wes."

I laugh. "Ooh, don't let her hear you say that."

We laugh together, and then I say, "Okay, I'll see you soon. We're almost there."

We say our goodbyes, and I shake my head. "I can't believe I found out like that."

"Right? I wish I hadn't been on," Shelli says, slipping her hand into mine. "She is super cute, and I love the name."

"I do too, really sweet. I want a girl now."

"What!" Shelli exclaims. "You said you wanted all boys."

"Yeah, but I think I changed my mind. She's so cute."

Shelli grins as she looks down at the photo of our niece. "She really is. Looks just like Asher. All that gorgeous dark hair."

"Not to sound cocky..." I start, and she laughs.

"Oh no, not you. Cocky? Please!"

I laugh. "But Fitz is a handsome son of a gun, and you know our girl would be gorgeous."

She grins. "I know, Aiden, but I am so busy right now. I don't want a stressful pregnancy."

"I get that, but I really want to knock you up."

She laughs again, the joy filling the car and making me hard everywhere. "You just like trying to score."

"I always score," I say with a wink. "But yes, I love practicing."

Her face fills with color. "So do I, but things are so wild right now. Let's revaluate this summer?"

I hold up a finger. "Or you can take some stuff off your plate, and we can get this going. We said we wanted the kids to be close like you and Posey." She nods, but I don't think she's listening to me. "Remember?"

She makes a face and then looks at me with her brow raised. Her eyes always get me. The color, the shape, the way her lashes fan, it all just blows me away. For so long, the love of my life was right under my nose. She is so stunningly beautiful and all mine. I get to love her, I get to grow old with her, and I get to watch her mother my children. But most of all, I get to be on the receiving end of that breathtaking gaze.

My wife.

"You okay?" I ask since I don't think she is.

With her brows furrowed, she says, "Piper Titov just posted a photo of the state of Tennessee with a heart over Nashville, and the caption reads, 'We're coming home this summer.'"

I don't understand. "Well, that's cool. Why do you have that face?"

"Because I was told they would never come home without the whole family. Which means..." Her voice drifts off, and her brows furrow more. "...Dimitri is coming with them."

I know I should know what she's talking about, but I really don't. "Okay?"

"He just posted a photo of himself in his dad's old Nashville

Assassins jersey with next season's start date on it. What the ever-loving fuck?" Before I can stop her, she's calling her mom. "Mom, what the hell? What do you mean? No, he won't just walk on the team. He's trash! What? How in the world do you make a promise like that when, hello, you do plan on retiring? Mom! Oh my God. I have a plan. This will mess with our salary cap. He isn't walking on. That's fine. We can discuss it Monday, but he isn't walking on. He will go to training camp, and River will know my feelings about how sloppy he is. His hands are weak, and he needs to gain about twenty pounds of muscle. Don't let this ruin our Christmas? Mom, I found out Asher and Ally had a baby on Instagram. Along with this, I am pissed. Don't people know how to use their phones for something more than social media? Whatever."

She throws down her phone and crosses her arms in a huff. I can feel the irritation rolling off her in waves. Before the words leave my mouth, I know I'm a dumbass. "So, where are we on baby-making?"

With fire in her eyes, Shelli glares at me. "Aiden, he is so fucking sloppy and has trash hands. The only reason he is successful in the KHL is because he is fast and can outskate anyone. Yes, he has a wicked trick shot, where he pops it up and then slaps it to the back of the net. But that won't work in the NHL because people are fast too and can catch him. Also, knock his ass into bum-fuck-tu! I am livid! How can she make these kinds of promises?"

I swallow hard. "Baby, she promised me I'd play for the Assassins."

"Because you are the best player out of all the Assassins kids!"

"Your brothers are good," I try, hopefully to calm her down. "And Odder."

"Oh my God, I could scream. I want to win. I don't want to keep twenty-year promises," she groans. "This is so stupid."

"Maybe send your mom a list of things he has to have before

training camp and see how it goes," I suggest since I really don't want this ruining our holiday.

She shakes her head. "She's going to fight for him, and she's not retired yet. She still has final say."

"Shelli, baby, this is months away. Don't let this ruin our trip. Your mom has gone out of her way to bring the whole family together. Let's leave this alone until Monday." I know my words are falling on deaf ears. She's spitting mad and I hate that, but I understand. I know how she spends her free time, watching tapes and studying stats. She is always on the phone with scouts. Hell, she's been scouting herself. She's dedicated and she's damn good at her job, but I don't want this negatively affecting our trip. "Nothing can be changed now. Elli won't go back on her word, so just keep doing you until this goes down. I know your mom, Shelli. She trusts you. Everything will be fine."

Shelli doesn't answer me. Instead, she leans her head on my shoulder and exhales hard. I kiss her temple, and neither of us says anything as I drive. I understand her frustration, but I also respect Elli's promises. She leads with her heart, while Shelli leads with her brain. I think the only time Shelli ever thought with her heart was when it came to me. With me, she threw all caution to the wind.

But with the Assassins, she's in it to win it. I want to win for her because of how hard she works and how much she loves the game of hockey. She's wicked smart when it comes to the sport, and while, yes, I am lucky enough to sleep with her, that doesn't sway my feelings that she's a great general manager. She is; she's a genius.

When she exhales hard again, I squeeze her thigh. "It will all work out."

"And even if it doesn't, it's okay," she says quietly. And that's something my wife wouldn't say. "I must stop with needing to have everything in my control. I am married to an incredible man, and I have an awesome son. We are going on a family vacation where we'll see everyone. And I'm over here upset over someone who's not even in this country, plus this stupid construction company, when I'm supposed to be on vacation."

"Exactly," I agree.

"How do you deal with me?"

I smile against her hair. "Oh, Shelli, it's easy. I love you."

She looks up at me as we stop at a light. I lean down, pressing my lips to hers. Our kiss is short but sends all the chills down my spine. "I love you too."

"Good. Can I knock you up again?"

She snorts with laughter, and I kiss her nose before the light turns green. "Now?"

I laugh. "Don't tempt me, woman. Fitz is sleeping, and I can pull over."

Her laughter is loud, and within seconds, Fitz is crying. She turns to put his pacifier back in his mouth, and I watch her in the mirror as she soothes him with her ass all up in air. I smack it playfully, and she laughs as she continues to appease our son. I wish she'd come appease me so I can knock her up with the next Brooks champion. And then another and another. All the babies. With Shelli Adler-Brooks, my world.

I Know

Emery

Stella combs her fingers through my hair before starting to French-braid my long, thick locks. Since she doesn't live with me anymore, I've been putting my hair up in a shower cap when I shower, and I hate it. I miss her doing my hair before my showers. I miss my sister. Which I know no one believes since we fight so badly, but she's low-key one of my favorite people. She's the one I want to be around and hang with. I feel protected with her. I'm not saying that Asher and Aiden aren't great, but they aren't Stella.

Nor are they someone else, but I am currently detoxing from said person, even though I am in a fucking chalet with him and his whole family. I didn't even enjoy seeing my new niece because I heard him coming into the house from skating. I ran out of that room like a cat from a room full of rocking chairs. I can't face him. Not yet. Ugh, I've made such a mess of things. Lost my sister to her hunky fiancé and lost my best friend because he's dumb and fell in love with me.

Stupid idiot.

I glance up to find Stella watching me in the mirror. God, why did you make her so pretty? Her sparkling gray eyes watch me knowingly as she perks her perfect brow at me. She's wearing some trendy, fashion-forward jumpsuit, looking all chic and cute. I look like I just crawled out of a trash can in a ratty old Assassins sweatshirt. I'm not even wearing pants because I was literally about to jump in the shower when she came in to greet me.

"So...our niece is adorable."

"Ah, small talk," I grumble, and she laughs. "Just be intrusive, Stel. It's the only way you know."

"That's not true. I'm a pro at small talk. I work in a restaurant." I roll my eyes as she grins at me. "Mom said you've been in rare form."

I shrug. "I have no clue what she is going on about."

"Dad told Wes you are basically the creature from *Stranger Things*, ready to eat everyone whole."

I would laugh if I weren't so annoyed. "Why is he telling Wes that? He's ruining my image."

Stella pauses. "And what image is that?"

I meet her gaze. "That I'm a joy and a delight."

Stella's face is blank. "You told Wes if he doesn't treat me right, you will kill him and dispose of the body without getting caught."

"This is true. That's part of my delight."

"And is the joy when you sent him a photo of the new coding system you made, in which you implied that you could erase who he is with one click if he hurts me?"

I think this over. "Sure. He needs to know."

"Did you do this to Shelli or Ally?"

I give her a wide grin. "No, 'cause I don't want them to see me coming."

"Emery! You look like a damn serial killer!" I know she says it to make me laugh, but I haven't laughed in a while.

Two weeks, to be exact.

When I don't laugh, she eyes me and then leans in, holding my hair at the base of my head. "What's going on, Em? Is it Quinn?"

I look down at my hands and shrug. "He's so dumb."

Her breath is warm against my skin as she asks, "Did he hurt you?"

I shake my head, hitting her cheek with mine. "No. I ghosted him."

"Why?"

I wring my fingers, squeezing them as I exhale hard. "It's stupid," I say, feeling dumb. "Or, I'm stupid. I don't know. We've been hooking up for a while now, like over a year. But I truly thought it was just that. Mindless, awesome sex, but remember when Craig, from my coding class, and I came into the restaurant a couple weeks ago?"

"Tall, lanky kid?"

"Yeah. Well, like, I kinda felt...I guess, guilty 'cause I accepted his invite. But then, I'm not with Quinn. Yes, we hang out a lot, but it isn't like we are saying I love you or making plans or anything like that. I mean, I don't want that."

"True. Plus, you're both very busy."

"Exactly. I truly thought it was just booty calls to blow off steam. We have a lot of fun..." I start, but then I trail off because I miss his body. When I say we had fun, we had fun. He doesn't know he was my first, but I know I was his, and I've enjoyed learning things with him. He's so caring, and God, I'd love to have one more time. Just one.

"But it was more to him?" she asks, pulling me from all my dirty memories.

I shrug. "I guess, because he was there when Craig and I walked in. I didn't know. But then he sent me a text, and we had a fight, and that's when I realized that it was. I got scared, so I ghosted him."

Stella holds my gaze. "Emery." Just my name has me so guilt-ridden. "We've known him forever. You should have done better than that."

I swallow hard. "I know, but..." But what? I don't know. I don't understand what I am feeling or even what I am thinking.

I am on the brink of launching my invention to different precincts. I just signed a contract to mass-produce my device for all across America, and it's my goal to continue my work by viewing the footage to help catch the bad guys. To see things the cops don't see and to help. I don't want to be a stiff in an office; I want to be behind the camera. Add in the fact that I'm in college, too, and it would be ridiculous for me to think I can have a relationship. Especially with someone who is starting his clinicals. A relationship isn't even what I want. I haven't traveled, and I'm not ready to be strapped to one person like my parents and my siblings are.

And that's exactly what would happen.

I'd be strapped to Quinn. I'd fall for him, and I'd be his for the rest of my life.

"I'm not ready for that." I look up at my sister. "He would be my Wes."

Stella's face changes as she moves her hand up my arm before continuing to braid. "Did you tell him that?"

"No. I didn't tell him anything. I just stopped talking to him."

"Emery, you know he's downstairs."

"I know. I'm hoping he'll just stay away from me."

She scoffs. "Maybe if you growl at him, he will."

I shake my head. "He isn't scared of me."

"Ah. So he is dumb."

I smile, which feels good as she pats my back. "You need to talk to him. Be honest."

I shrug. "I'd rather not."

She squeezes my shoulder. "I know." She kisses the top of my head before getting off the bed. "But you would kill him if he ghosted you."

She isn't wrong, and I hate that. "I missed you before this."

She winks at me. "I miss you more, sis."

Stella walks out of the room, shutting the door behind her. I look in the mirror, taking in my beautifully braided hair and my tired expression. I've lost sleep over Quinn, and I know it's because what Stella said is right. I need to speak to him and give him some closure, but I don't want closure. I selfishly want to leave the door wide open for the future, but that's not fair. Quinn is a gem, and any girl would be lucky to be on the receiving end of his love. A girl who is ready.

I hate her, and she doesn't even exist.

I get off the bed and grab my toiletries bag before heading into the attached bathroom. Only Elli Adler would get a chalet like this, with bathrooms so big that three rooms are connected to it. It's kinda crazy and over the top, but that's Elli Adler. As I lock the door to the very small room off to the side, I can't decide if it's a nursery or a weird-ass office. Maybe a closet. It doesn't even have a door to the hallway. Weird. I turn on my heel and head to the other door. But before I can get there, a rather large, shirtless male stops midstep in the doorway.

I freeze as Quinn's gaze meets mine, and I swear this crazy shit only happens in crappy rom-com movies—and my life.

The fuck?

But for real, why does he have to be so sexy?

I don't know many doctors who have time to work out, but Quinn does, and his body shows it. Ripples of muscles and shoulders that are meant to be bitten. He used to be skinny and small, but then he hit puberty and became this masterpiece. I went through puberty, bled for a solid two weeks, and broke out everywhere. Not Quinn. Nope. He got sexy. I tell myself not to look anywhere but his eyes, even though his eyes are dangerous, but of course, my eyes move along his body to find he's in only a towel.

Well. Fuck. Me.

My fingers bite into my bag as I meet his gaze again. Neither of us moves, nor do we speak as we hold each other's gaze. His blue eyes are so tender, so bright, and concerned. He slowly slips his tongue out of his mouth, wetting his lips, and I swear to God, I almost explode.

I miss that mouth.

"I didn't know Stella was here."

I bring in my brows. "What?"

"She braided your hair, I assume?"

Instantly, I move my hand to my hair, which makes my shirt rise up, and I watch as he takes an eyeful. Heat blazes through us, my heart starts to pound, and my skin starts to tingle. "Ugh, yeah. Um—"

"I love your hair like that," he admits shyly. "It always reminds me of..."

His voice trails off because he doesn't have to say it. Our first time together, my hair was in a tight braid that Stella had done before I left for Boston. I'd had no intention of hooking up with Quinn. We had always been close friends and got along great.

It was late one night; we were up playing video games and high on sugar. He admitted he was still a virgin, and I decided I wanted him to be my first. Quinn has always made me feel safe and has always been there for me. It seemed only natural for me to want that. And now, as I gaze at him, I know why.

Because our bodies yearn for each other.

"Yeah," I say softly, and then I jerk my thumb behind me. "Um, I guess I'll go so you can take a show—" My sentence is cut off when he wraps his hand around my wrist. He's suddenly in front of me, towering over me in all his beautiful glory. I swallow hard as I feel the heat of him spread over me in waves. He brings his other hand up, taking my jaw and running his thumb along my chin. I feel the towel hit my bare feet, and I gasp, breathless.

"Quinn, I don't think this is a good idea," I whisper. I'm not sure if I'm saying that for him or for me.

His eyes burn into mine. Gone is the concern, replaced by the same hot lust that has me quivering between my thighs. "I miss you, E." Quinn drops his head, just enough so that his lips are at my cheek. I take in a quick breath, feeling every inch of him against my thigh. His lips are warm, soft against my cheek as he says, "I miss you so much, it hurts."

My eyes drift shut, and if anyone asks, I blacked out.

Or better yet, I didn't have control of my body.

I rise on my toes, turning my face so our lips meet. He drops his hand from my wrist and takes me around my waist, pulling me off my feet and into his hard, burning body. I go willingly, wantonly, and wrap my arms around his neck. Our kisses are demanding and feel as if they're desperate. Maybe they are, because I feel like if I don't kiss him, I'll cry. His lips fit with mine in a way I've never experienced. He tastes like cocoa and peppermint. Quinn holds me, and I hear the door shut and then lock. He turns and sits me on the counter, stepping between my legs and taking my face in his hands. He strokes my cheeks as he draws the kisses from me. Sucking on my bottom lip, he bites softly, causing me to cry out in longing. I run my fingers up the ripples of his back to his shoulders, where I dig my nails into his flesh as I move to the edge of the counter. I feel his cock between my thighs, throbbing, and I want to scream out in joy. He slides his mouth from mine, kissing my chin, my jaw, before sucking my earlobe into his mouth. I gasp, arching into him, and once more, my body isn't mine. I find myself rubbing my body against him like we're here to cop a quick feel, but I know neither of us could have only that. He groans against my neck and then bites ever so gently. I squeeze his shoulder, slowly stroking him with my panty-clad pussy. His hands are shaking against my ass, and the sounds he makes are music to my ears. He starts to guide my ass slowly, so fucking slow it hurts, along him, and both of us are shaking with want.

I swear on everything holy, I'm about to come undone.

"I can't fucking handle you."

"Same," I say harshly, breathlessly.

He pulls back, his face red and his eyes so damn threatening, I know I should be scared, but instead, I'm excited. Quinn takes my panties in his hands and yanks them off. His mouth parts as he takes me in, and I'm blinded by desire. He slips his hands up under me and lifts me. I wrap my arms and legs around his head as my back slams into the wall by the door. I bite into my lip to keep from screaming as he buries his face in my pussy. His tongue comes out, finding my entrance, and fucks me like he would with his dick. His hands squeeze my thighs, my ass, as I writhe against the wall. I'm not even worried about falling. He has me, and I'm about to come so fucking hard, I couldn't care less if I die after.

His nose presses into my clit as he sucks and licks me all over. I grip his hair, my thighs squeezing his head as he continues his glorious assault on me. He moves his head up, finding my clit with his mouth, and it doesn't take long before I'm gone. I convulse against his mouth, arching off the wall so hard, he stumbles back, but he holds me like I weigh nothing. My release shakes me to my core, and I can feel him everywhere as he uses the wall to slowly lower me down.

Onto his cock.

I open my eyes in shock at how easy that was, to find him smiling from ear to ear. I can't help but laugh. Loudly. His eyes brighten as he covers my mouth with his, swallowing my laughter. He holds me so close, our kisses getting hotter by the second. I squeeze his hips with my thighs as he holds me by my ass. I clutch his shoulders, rubbing them with my thumbs until he wraps his arm around me, using his other to pull at my shirt. I help him take it off, and his deep, throaty groan tells me he loves that I don't have a bra on.

He kisses me between my breasts and then takes a mouthful of one, awakening all my desire once more. I feel Quinn throbbing, and my legs start to quake. He licks my nipple, flicking his tongue along it before he starts to move inside me. Each thrust is harder and deeper than the last. His eyes are lost with desire, and soon, I'm holding on so I don't go through the wall. I feel him everywhere, and when he comes, it's with a yell I have missed more than I would ever admit. He presses me into the wall, and I wrap my arms and legs around him once more. He gasps against my skin as I do the same, seeing lights behind my eyelids. Every part of me is on fire, and I swear, I'm more confused than I've ever been.

Seconds turn to minutes, and then slowly, he moves his lips along my collarbone and then up my neck to my jaw. I enjoy his nibbles on my neck for a second, but then I stop him for a long, lusty kiss. He takes my jaw in his hand and gazes into my eyes. I know what he is about to say before he even says it.

"I love you, E."

My heart kicks into action and wants me to scream the words back at him, but instead, I whisper, "I know."

Something moves in his eyes, but before either of us can dwell on my response, I take his lips with mine.

To distract us from what my heart wants but my mind knows I'm not ready for.

Not in a Festive Mood

POSEY

Boon slides his thumb along the back of my hand, softly and with such tenderness. Neither of us has moved since we pulled up to the cabin. Oh, I mean chalet. When I called it a cabin to Shelli, she quickly corrected me. I guess the massiveness of the house does deserve a pretty word like chalet. Not that I care. Not that I want to be here. Boon moves in and kisses my jaw.

He's been a godsend, but then again, from the moment I met Boon, I knew he was special. His support is bar none, and his love for me is inspiring. I never thought I'd find someone like my mom found my dad, but here I am, living out my own love story. Unfortunately, unlike my parents, Boon and I have a few gut-wrenching chapters in our story.

"Lovely, we can go back home. We don't have to stay. I'm sure Elli will understand."

I don't answer him at first. I only shrug as the tears sting my eyes. "I'm fine."

"Posey, you don't have to be strong around me."

I look over at him and meet his gaze. "The last thing I feel right now is strong, Boon."

His shoulders fall as he squeezes my hand. "You are the strongest woman I know, and I love you, lovely. So damn much."

I swallow hard as I nod, and then I push the door open. The snow crunches under my feet as I stand, ignoring the pain I feel. I move to open the back door, and Zac looks right up at me from his car seat. His eyes light up, his toothy grin filling me with such joy as I smile back at him. "Hello, my love. Are you just waking up? Look at that wide smile for Mama." I kiss him all over as I unbuckle his car seat. I reach for the large blanket beside him and wrap him up. I know that Boon gets mad at me for not putting him in a coat, but I am terrified of the car seat with Zac in a coat. Shelli calls me a helicopter mom, but I know for a fact that she'll turn into one too.

We were raised by one.

I shut the door with my foot and walk around to the rear of the car as the snow falls on us. Zac laughs loudly as I playfully try to catch snowflakes with my tongue. "Me, me!" he yells, and he mimics me as Boon watches with a smile on his face. We meet at the back to get our bags.

"You have a good nap, bud? That was a long trip, huh?"

"Dadadadadadada," Zac squeals, reaching for him. Boon takes him, along with our bags, as I reach for the bag with the presents. When I reach for it, I realize totally forgot that I put our sign in the car when my mom was coming over the other day. It's just a simple wooden sign, but it might as well be neon, flashing and making a siren noise. I can't stop staring at it.

Baby number 2. Coming this summer!

We were going to have Zac carry it in, but that won't be happening. I feel Boon's eyes on me before he comes up beside me. He sees what I'm looking at and exhales heavily. "Come on, lovely," he whispers, taking the bag of presents from me. "Your mom is wondering where you are."

I don't move, though. I just keep staring at the sign. "It's not fair."

"It isn't."

"This one was supposed to stick."

He nods, leaning into me and kissing my jaw. "I know." Boon kisses my cheek and then my nose. "But we have an appointment to meet with the doctors after the new year, and we'll see what's going on."

"What if I'm unable to keep a pregnancy?"

He touches his forehead to mine. "Posey, don't go straight to the worst case. Let's wait to see what the doctors say."

"I want another baby," I whisper, and I don't even realize I'm crying until he wipes my tears away. "I feel like I'm failing you."

"Posey," he says sternly. "Never."

"But you want a huge family."

He forces me to look into his eyes. "No. I want you. Everything else is a bonus." I swallow hard, and he kisses my lips. "You give me everything I could ever need and more, Posey."

I nod slowly as I lean into him. "I love you."

He kisses my nose. "I love you," he whispers, and then he takes my hand. "Come on. It looks like Santa threw up Christmas in there."

My lips quirk as I nod. "It's her favorite season."

"Yeah, where is my Christmas skit, like last year?"

I grin. "Not happening. In her defense, she made sure the chalet was ready."

He sighs. "Great."

Boon wraps his arm around me, and we walk in together. To complete chaos. Which, really, isn't surprising. Pretty sure the only person we're missing is God himself. Though, if you ask my mom, he's already here. I walk around with a fake smile on my face and greet all my family. The Brookses are here and the Titovs. When I get to my aunt Grace, she kisses my nose and hugs me tightly.

I can smell the wine on her breath. "So, you've been drinking all day?"

She nods. "Your mom stresses me out, and I haven't gotten laid in six months."

"There is an app for that," I suggest, but then our billet kid, Benson, raises his hand.

"I will totally take one for the team. You're hot, Aunt Grace."

Grace looks at me with such shock on her face that I can't help but laugh. She leans in and asks, "Is it wrong if I take him up on it? I know it will be like dirty old lady cougar stuff, but I'm pretty sure he'd be using me to get over that girl who broke his heart."

I'm unsure if we're all supposed to know about what happened with Benson and his friend Cam, but our family can't keep their mouths shut. I know how upset he is and how he wishes she wouldn't have cut off all communication with him.

I just wish it were easy to get over stuff like that. But when your heart is involved, it's not that simple. Which is why my aunt Grace is still completely in love with my uncle James, even after his being gone for over ten years now.

Thankfully, before she can take Benson up on his offer, her son Ryan and his wife Sofia walk in. They are so beautiful together, and both are thriving. Sofia's gym is such a success, and all the videos she posts on TikTok are fun to see. I love getting to see Ryan at the rink and working closely with him. But what I'm not ready for is the belly that Sofia is holding in her hands.

They're pregnant.

Finally.

Grace lets out a shriek and wraps her arms around her first-born and his wife. I've been waiting for them to have kids; I just wish I weren't so sad about my own loss. I feel Boon's gaze on me, but I don't want him to be worried about me. I'm operating on autopilot, hugging and congratulating them. I move out of the way and back into a rather large body. I know instantly it's not Boon, and when I turn, I find it's Asher. He's got a huge smile on his face, and in his arms is a bundle of pink. A baby with his nose. I bring in my brows, and his grin just grows.

"Surprise! Alexis, this is your auntie Posey!"

I feel like I've been hit in the gut. "Wait, what?"

"We had a baby," he says, the image of the proud papa if I've ever seen one. My lips start to quiver as I gaze at the sweet little baby, and my heart hurts. I stroke my fingers along her cheek. "She's utterly perfect."

"Thanks. You're not mad, are you? Everyone is mad we hid it."

I swallow back my emotion. "Not at all. I'm just so happy for you," I somehow say. "I'm sorry. I'm not in a festive mood. Excuse me."

I kiss her little head and then Asher's cheek and head for the door. I must get out of here. Right this fucking second. I look for Boon, and he has Zac on his hip, laughing with Grace and my dad. I slip out the back door, and the cool air is welcoming. I stare out at the top of the mountain, and I'm in awe of its beauty. I swallow past the sob in my throat and look around for somewhere to go. I kind of want to be alone. I love my husband, but he's been very suffocating since we left the hospital a couple days ago. It seems like it's been years rather than days.

When my eyes fall on a bright purple-and-black Tuff box, I know it's our family ice-skating stuff from home. Dad used to bring it with us when we'd go north to visit family. I crunch through the snow toward the frozen pond where the box is. I take in the huge ADLER name written on top and then all of our first names around it. We all signed the box when we learned to spell our names. Dad put sealant over the names so they'd never come off.

Of course, Shelli's name has a heart over her i. Mine is under my dad's name, with my old hockey number. Owen and Evan are right next to each other, while Quinn is over by my mom. I smile as I trace my finger along the names. I remember everyone signing this box and how we'd all get ready for family hockey games during the holidays in Boston. Those are some of my favorite memories. Our family. Together.

I want to make my own memories with a big family like the one I grew up in. God, Zac is so lucky. He is completely and utterly loved by the greatest people. Yes, his aunt is a drama queen and his twin uncles are unpredictable and Quinn probably doesn't even know Zac exists, but Mom and Dad are the best. They make up for all these crazy siblings they gave me. I open the box and find my skates. I pull them out and then sit on a huge log to put them on. Maybe burning my thighs will make me feel better. I know I need to take it easy, but I've been skating since before I walked, so I'm fine.

As I get my first skate on, I hear the crunching of snow, and I look up to see my dad coming toward me. He puts on his gloves and hollers, "You got it?"

I grin. I've been putting on skates for a long time, but my dad tying up my skates is nine times better than me. "Nope."

He laughs as he bends down in front of me. "I figured you didn't." He makes fast work of my skates and then pats my calves. "All done."

"Thanks, Dad."

I don't move, though, as he sits beside me. He exhales, and I smile as I take him in. It's weird to look at him and know he's a granddad. To my baby.

"You gonna tell me what's going on?" he asks as he reaches for his skates that are conveniently on the top. Mine were at the bottom. "I see it all over your face, Pose. So, just tell me."

I swallow hard. "I miscarried Sunday."

His shoulders fall, and I know he's taken back to the tubal pregnancy I almost died from. "Are you okay?"

"I guess. It didn't have a heartbeat when we went in for imaging."

"Fuck, baby. I'm sorry."

40

I lean into my hero and close my eyes. "This is the second one this year."

I feel him tense up, and then he wraps his arms around me, kissing my temple. "Pose, I'm sorry. Have you told Mom?"

I shake my head. "No. The first one was at like eight weeks, so I didn't want anyone feeling bad for me. And it's the same for this one. It just sucks."

"It does, and it's bullshit."

"Agreed," I say, and he hugs me tight.

"I won't say anything."

I laugh. "Dad, I fully expect Mom to crawl into my bed tonight after you tell her."

He grins against my temple. "No, I won't. Though, she'll want to comfort you when she finds out."

"Boon is already being so supportive and loving. It's overwhelming 'cause I feel like I'm failing him."

Dad gives me a look. "Posey, that boy is lucky I let him marry you."

I grin. "Dad, stop."

"You're an absolute gem, Posey. No one is good enough for you," he says, kissing me once more. "But Boon is growing on me. I like him okay."

I grin, hugging him tightly. "I love him."

"Yeah. I was at the wedding."

Our gazes meet, and my heart swells. I love my dad. "You know you're the best dad, right?"

He winks. "'Cause you're the best daughter." He kisses me again then lets me go to start tying his skates. When he looks back up at me with a sheepish grin, I have to laugh. "Don't tell Shelli I said that."

We share a laugh and then head to where hockey sticks are stabbed into the snow. We each grab one and then take turns shooting into the old goal Dad brought from home. After I take a shot, I notice my brothers trudging through the snow, and I groan.

"Ew, Dad, make the boys go away," I whine like I used to when I was younger.

They laugh as Dad looks back at me. "There is enough ice for all of us."

"I swear you've been saying that since they were born," I accuse, and he laughs. With his eyes bright, his nose red, and a grin on his face, he skates over to me, wrapping his arms around me. He hugs me close and then whispers in my ear.

"And you'll say it to your babies. I know you will." He squeezes me. "No matter how they come, Posey. Whether you carry them or you adopt them, no matter what, we'll love them as we love you. You are so strong, so incredible, and so beautiful. I am so proud you're mine."

When he pulls back and our eyes meet, I can feel my eyes clouding. God gave me the ultimate gift by making him my dad. I don't know what my future holds, but one thing is for sure, I am loved and supported. Under my dad's loving gaze, my heart isn't aching as bad anymore. How could it be when I am loved by the three best men in the world?

Zac, Boon, and my daddy.

My year-round Christmas gifts.

Every Inch

OWEN

I haul ass to the puck, and even though Evan hasn't been on the ice much, he gives me a run for it. Evan has always been swifter than me. I have the brawn, as my mom says, and Evan has the speed. I'm sure my teammates would say that's why they miss him. But for me, I miss my other half. Evan somehow beats me, but I may have let him win for the pure fact that I'm almost coming out of my skin with excitement that he's on the ice with me.

It's been a long time since we've done this, and while I gave my mom shit for putting all of us in a house together with other families for Christmas, I know if she hadn't, I wouldn't have this moment with my family. A game on a frozen pond with huge mountains surrounding us and nothing but pure competition on the ice.

He passes the puck between his legs to our dad, who carries it up the ice to where Quinn stands in as goalie. Since there isn't a goalie bone—or hell, even a hockey bone—in our baby brother's body, and Dad is a beast, he scores easily. Quinn glares as Dad,

Posey, and Evan tease him relentlessly, but I just grin, not caring one bit that they're kicking Shelli's, Aiden's, and my asses. You'd think with two star hockey players, we'd be sweeping them. But Posey is damn good, Shelli isn't, and Dad scares us all. Oh, and I don't think anyone really wants to truly compete against Evan since we're all just happy he's on the ice.

Mom scolds everyone as she holds a huge cup of hot chocolate, shivering but not giving up on the game. I wish she'd play, but she complains her hip isn't the same. I blame it on those heels she wears; I know that's why Shelli isn't good anymore. She traded her skates for her heels and hasn't looked back. Tragic, really.

Beside my incredible mom is my girl, my everything, my Angie. I skate toward her, and when her eyes meet mine, my grin widens even more. Her hair is down under the large beanie that almost covers her eyes. Her face is red and I can tell she's cold, but I don't think she wants to be inside with all the craziness going on there. Everyone is in stitches over Asher and Ally's new baby. I don't know how they keep things a secret, but I swear, Asher has been doing that since the beginning. I guess he and Evan are cut more from the same cloth than Evan and I, because Evan has been keeping it a secret that he is going to propose to his girl since May, I think.

I don't get it. When I knew I wanted to marry Angie, I said yes since she beat me to the question. I couldn't wait. I called Mom and Dad five minutes after she asked. When I thought I had knocked her up, I was ready to call my parents the moment the test came back. Yeah, I was scared, and I knew we weren't ready for kids, but I couldn't wait to tell everyone. Even with the test coming back negative, I still wanted to tell my parents there had been a moment I'd thought Angie was pregnant. I don't know, maybe I'm overly proud of my relationship.

With one hell of a woman.

"I don't know how he beat me," I say, and she laughs as she

leans over the makeshift fence to kiss me. I kiss her eagerly, our kiss warming me up a bit.

"He's always been faster," she says, fixing the collar of my shirt. I just threw a hoodie on and didn't worry about the collar of my undershirt at all. "But you're way hotter."

"Hey!" Callie protests, and Angie laughs. "My man is super hot."

"Some would say they're identical," Mom teases, and I grin back at her.

"No one says that but you, Mom," I remind her, and everyone laughs as the rest of my family gathers around. Evan skates to where Callie is, and man, it makes me really happy to see him so happy. I don't think I can ever thank Callie enough for how she helped save my brother. His mental health has been so much better since she came along. It isn't cured, not that I think you can cure mental illness, but he's better. He's maintaining his meds, and he's skating. After not being able to—for almost a year. For me, that's winning.

Angie leans over the fence thingy and wraps her arms around my waist. I kiss the top of her head before stabbing my stick into the snow. I wrap my arms around her as Mom says, "Hey, I think your parents are here."

We all turn to where a car is pulling in. Angie doesn't move, though, and I hate how nervous she is. She has "gained weight," as she tells me, but I don't see it. All I see is my gorgeous, thick, sexy queen, and it kills me how she is letting her weight define every-thing. She says she pushed the wedding back because of a dress that wasn't available until Christmas, but I think it's because she hasn't met her "goal" weight. She frustrates me, but damn if I don't love her.

I look over to where her beautiful mom is getting out of the car, waving excitedly at us. Mom and Dad start for them as everyone else begins to pick up the sticks and equipment. We were waiting on the Paxton family to arrive for us to eat dinner. I kiss

Angie's head when I hear her groan. I look over to notice that her younger sister Charlotte is carrying a white dress bag.

The dress.

"We can't leave, can we?"

"Angie, baby, what's wrong? You've been excited about the dress."

She doesn't say anything or even look at me as she holds on to me. "I don't want to try it on and have it not fit."

"If it doesn't, we get a new size. It's a sample anyway, isn't it?"

"Yeah, but I don't want to disappoint my mom. And Lord knows Charlotte could fit it."

I take her neck in my hand, using my thumb to position her face to look at me. "Angie, Charlotte is a teenager. You're a whole-ass, fucking gorgeous woman. You can't compare yourself to her. You two aren't even in the same league."

"You're saying that because you love me."

"Well, duh, and because it's the truth."

"It's just... I know I'm supposed to be skinnier, Owen. Look at my mom."

I don't, though; my gaze stays on her. "Only you have my eye, Angie. Only you."

Her shoulders fall, and her face relaxes. She rises up on her toes to kiss me sweetly, and I relish her kiss. As we part, I kiss her top lip and then her nose. "That dress doesn't matter, Ang. The only thing that matters is you and me. I'd literally marry you right now, right here. I don't care about dresses, about who is there. I just want you."

Angie's eyes soften as she glides her thumb along my chin. "First, our moms would kill us. And second, I thought you wanted the wedding."

I scoff. "Ang, I'd marry you in our gym wear. Honestly. In a gym, baby. I don't care. I really don't. I just want to be married to you, so that when I knock you up, it's within wedlock and I'll stay my grandma's favorite."

She giggles as she holds my gaze. "Owen, baby, you know Evan is the favorite."

I give her a dry look. "No, I am sure it's me." Her eyes dance with mine, and I kiss her nose. "Am I your favorite?"

She grins. "Always."

Her lips meet mine, and I hold her a bit tighter than I was. The wind picks up and burns my face as we part. Our eyes lock, and I can't help but smile. I love my life because she's in it. "So, are we waiting till summer to get married, or should I get someone to be ordained?"

She laughs before whispering, "We're waiting because Evan is proposing."

"Oh yeah," I say, looking over to where Evan is kissing Callie. "Think he'll do it?"

She shrugs. "I don't see why he wouldn't. He has Nico's blessing."

"Reluctant blessing, and to be honest, no one would keep me from marrying you," I say with a cheesy grin that gets me a deep laugh.

"You've made this well known, Owen Adler, and guess what?"

"What?" I ask as she leans into me.

"Same. You're all mine."

Before I can take her and hide her away for some serious loving, I'm interrupted by my stupid little brother. "Gag, get a room."

I glare. "Go beg Emery to date you," I throw at him, and he just laughs.

"Dude, that's a done deal. We're already back together."

I snort. "Sure you are, buddy. Keep telling yourself that, because we all know you couldn't nail that girl down if you were a hammer and she was a nail."

"Har-har-har, loser," he throws back at me as he walks away with Benny beside him.

"Why are you mean to him? You know how he feels about her." Angie tsks me, and I give her a dark, playful look.

"Yes, and I also know how I feel when I'm interrupted from having my woman."

"You're impossible."

"I am," I agree, gathering her in my arms. "Impossibly in love with every single inch of you." Her lips tip up at the side as she cups my cheek. "Like, for real, if that dress doesn't fit, who the hell cares. Walk down the aisle naked, Angie," I say, and she laughs, her eyes so bright. "Your dad might get mad and everyone will get a show, but I'll be waiting for you."

She cups my face with her other hand and leans her head into mine. "Thank you for loving me."

"You make it easy," I promise, and she scoffs.

"I don't," she whispers, running her thumbs along my jaw. "Somehow, though, you won't give up on me."

"Never. When I love, I love for life. Ask Evan."

She grins. "He's a part of you. You're twins."

"And you're a part of me. My whole heart is yours."

Her eyes get glossy, and then she shakes her head. "I can't stand you. You lay it on so damn thick to the point that I have no clue what to say!"

I laugh. "Just tell me your truth, 'cause all this is mine."

Her eyes lock with mine. "I love you, Owen. With my whole being."

I lean in, pressing my lips to hers, though not for a kiss. Instead, I say, "Same, baby. Same."

I kiss her then, and as the wind and snow swirl around us, not a single inch of me is cold. Not when I have Angie Paxton, soon-to-be Adler, in my arms.

A Thousand, Million, Trillion Times, Yes

Callie

I haven't really seen or spoken to Benny since everything happened with my best friend, Cameron. I think they tried to date, but I get the feeling too much went down too quickly. Then Cameron went home for the summer, and communication stopped between them. In the gym, I've found myself asking her if she's spoken to Benny, but she never really answers me. She just skirts around it and then goes to a different event from me. I know she knows she made the right choice for her, and even for Benny, but I think he scares her. I think she saw a future with him, and that wasn't what she wanted.

Right guy, wrong time.

I hope that's the case, because I do really like him.

"I thought you were going home?" Evan says, but Benny shakes his head.

"No, my mom is acting weird. I'd rather be here with you guys than them. Just a bunch of bullshit family stuff."

"Well, we're glad you're here," I say softly, patting his arm, and he nods.

Visibly uncomfortable, Benny asks, "Have you spoken to Cameron?"

I knew he was going to ask, and still, I have no clue what to say. "Yeah, this morning. She's doing well."

"That's good. Real good." He shoots me a forgiving smile. "Not trying to put you in the middle of our drama."

"Nothing like the drama of Dimitri Titov coming back, huh, sis?" Owen says, leaning on the island as Shelli glares at him. I love Owen, I do, but man, he knows how to get under his siblings' skin.

"You are not funny," she seethes, and even Mrs. Adler shoots him a dark look. "Mom and I have decided to wait until we're in the office to discuss this."

Owen just grins, ear to ear. "Okay. I'm just saying there is drama because you hate him and he is going to play for you."

"I don't hate him," Shelli says. Though, to me, it looks like she does.

"She does," Evan says under his breath. "They have never gotten along."

"Why?" I ask. "Isn't he kinda related to you?"

"In the six degrees of the Assassins?" Evan asks, and I laugh. "Yes, but they have never been able to see eye to eye. He could say the sky was blue, and Shelli would argue with him."

I grin back at her but promptly quit when I find her mad as hell. "Dimitri has no control over my emotions like that. I don't argue with stupidity."

"You argue with the twins all the time," Posey says, popping a tomato into her mouth. The twins flip her the bird, and she laughs as she leans on the counter too. "He won't last. He's played too rough for too long. He won't be able to clean up. Mom is doing this as a favor to a friend."

"Dimitri is quick, though, has a good shot," Owen says. "He always has."

"I'm telling you, he won't make the roster," Posey says, and Boon bounces Zac beside her.

"You never know. People never thought I'd make roster, and I did."

She looks up at her husband. "That's because you're amazing. Dimitri is not."

Shelli points to her sister. "See? I'm not the only one who doesn't like him."

Evan snorts. "She doesn't like him 'cause you don't."

Posey shakes her head. "No. He's always been very 'I'm better than you.' A jackass."

"Who, Dimitri?" Angie asks, coming to stand beside Owen. She's holding Asher's new baby. "Yeah, total jackass. He had a goal to sleep with all the Assassins daughters, and when I found out, I laid him out on the ice."

Owen glances over at his fiancée and gives her a look. "Why didn't I know this?"

"Because of that face right there. It was eons ago. I'm marrying you," she says then hands the baby off to him. "Matter of fact, I'm about to go try on my dress. Callie, wanna join?"

I smile widely. I love that I have a relationship with Angie. At first, she was super reserved. But now, we're basically besties. We text a lot, and we are always together when Evan and I are back in South Carolina. The goal is for us to move there when we graduate. I'll work at my home gymnastics center, and if Nico hasn't killed Evan yet, Evan will work in the center that Nico is opening.

Just the thought of my pseudo-father has me rolling my eyes. He has been so hateful the last couple weeks. I don't get it. He says he likes Evan just fine, but any time I bring him up, he gets so testy. I know he hates that I'm growing up and that I'm living my own life. It must be because he wants to protect me. After everything that happened with my bio dad, then Aviva's cancer stuff, and all my issues, I know he is only doing it out of love. But man, he can be very suffocating.

When I feel everyone staring at me, I look around and say, "Oh! Yes, I'd love to. Sorry, I started daydreaming."

I flash Evan a grin and then fall into step with Angie on the way to the back room where her mom is unzipping the dress bag. Her sister, Charlotte, sits on the bed with Mrs. Brooks. Everyone is so excited. I glance at Angie, and she gives me a nervous look. I reach out, cupping her wrist. "It's okay," I mouth, and she swallows hard.

"Thanks," she whispers, and I really don't understand how she doesn't look in the mirror and see how beautiful she is. Her body is killer. Thick in all the right places. I love her figure, and I'm sure when I'm not in the gym anymore, I'll look a lot like her. Strong arms, thick biceps, and a tummy, with big legs and ass. I know she is nervous about trying on this dress with her skinny momma and sister, but how can she not see how much they love her?

My phone rings just as I sit down. It's Aviva, my sister.

"Excuse me," I say, and Angie waves me off as I answer the FaceTime. "Hey!"

Aviva's face is not happy. "You did not text, nor call, when you got there."

"Oh! My bad. Evan started playing hockey on this pond here, and I got distracted."

"I almost called Mrs. Adler."

Everyone starts to tease me with "Ooh, you're in trouble," but I keep my focus on my sister. "I'm sorry. Like I said, we got here, and things have been busy. I am sorry."

"I'll forgive you," she decides. "What are you doing?"

"Angie is about to try on her dress!" I say excitedly, and Aviva grins.

"Awesome. Send me pictures if you can. Oh, and someone wants to tell you goodnight," she says, and then I see my squishy nephew.

"Merry Christmas!" he exclaims. "Santa is coming!"

"He is! I can't wait to see what you get! What do you think it is?"

He taps his little chin. His beautiful eyes are bright and full of magic. "A dog."

I snort. "Buddy, remember, Santa can't bring a dog. He doesn't want to squish him in his bag."

My sweet baby pouts. "Fine, a bike."

"Ohh, I bet that might be what Santa brings. Will you call me in the morning?"

He nods quickly and then blows me a kiss. I do the same as Aviva comes back on the phone. "Where is Evan?"

I shrug. "Out with his family. We're in the back room so Angie can try on the dress."

"Nice. Okay. Um... Okay. I guess, just call me tomorrow?"

I make a face at the way she's acting. "Yeah, I will, weirdo."

She laughs. "Love ya, kid."

"Love you."

I hang up, thinking that was strange, but Aviva can be odd. I look up just as Angie comes out of the bathroom with the dress held up with her hands. I can tell why she wanted to move her wedding to the summertime. This dress is pure lace. It hugs her curves in a mermaid style that fans out around her. I'm in awe as Fallon and Lucy start to tie up the back.

"I don't know why you were worried it wouldn't fit, love. It's a corset back," her mom says, tying it up. The dress has a deep V front, and it sparkles as she moves.

When we hear a knock at the door, we all look back as Mrs. Adler comes in. Her jaw drops as she clasps her hands in front of her chest. "Oh, Angela. You're stunning."

"Isn't she!" Lucy says, wiping her cheeks. "Gorgeous."

I watch as Angie slowly looks up into the mirror, her expression so unsure. She runs her hands along her body, pulling at the fabric and then making a face. I know for a fact she's picking herself apart.

"You look awesome, Angie," I say, but I don't think she hears me.

"Do you not like it?" Charlotte asks, and Angie shrugs.

"Maybe if I lose twenty more pounds? You think?" she asks her mom, but before Lucy can answer, Mrs. Adler holds up her hand.

"Angela, look at yourself. You are perfect the way you are. You wear that dress, just as you are, and Owen will probably pass out at the altar."

Angie looks back over her shoulder at Mrs. Adler. "I could be thinner."

Mrs. Adler snorts. "So could I, and you don't see me waiting to be a specific size to live my life."

Angie presses her lips together.

"Do you love the dress?"

Angie slowly looks back at herself, nodding. "It's a beautiful dress, my dream dress."

Elli nods. "Do you love my son?"

Angie turns then. "Yes, of course I do."

"Do you want to marry him?"

"Yes."

"The dress fits?"

"Yes, ma'am."

"Then, what's the issue?"

Lucy slips her hand in her daughter's. "She's right. You're perfectly made, my love."

"You are," I say softly. "Truly."

Angie glides her hands back down the dress and turns to look at herself in the mirror. I can see the doubt creeping back in, and playfully, I say, "I can go get Owen. He'll tell ya."

Everyone laughs, but I can tell she wants that. She meets my gaze, and she doesn't have to say a word. I get up, even though her mom and Owen's start to complain.

"He can't see her in her dress!"

I don't care. If she wants Owen, I'm getting Owen. I head

down the hall, calling for him. He appears out of nowhere, and I laugh. "Angie needs you to reassure her. She's doubting how she looks."

"Fucking hell. Thanks," he says, and then Evan pops his head out of the door that Owen had just come in from. I cock my head at him in confusion, and he looks kind of crazy. A red nose, wild eyes, and wind-kissed cheeks.

"What in the world are you doing?"

"We found a Bigfoot track."

I snort hard. "Evan, stop."

"No, for real. Come on. You got your phone? That's what Owen was getting."

"Wait, are you serious?"

"Yes. Come on," he urges, and he helps me get my hat and coat on. I put on my gloves and step into my snow boots with his assistance. He takes my hand, and we head out into the darkness.

"How in the hell did you find a track?" I ask as he uses my phone for light. There is some light from the moon and then the massive number of Christmas lights Elli had put up, but it's still dark.

"We were out here getting the sticks, and I found it. It's crazy!" he says, laughing, almost as if he doesn't believe it himself. "Remember last year when we went through Bigfoot country?"

I smile widely at him. "Of course I do. How could I ever forget that?" I ask, and honestly, how could I? Our love story is, of course, my favorite. I mean, don't get me wrong, my sister's is great, and I got a dad and a nephew out of it, but Evan? Well, Evan's love has been life-changing. I never knew I could love someone the way I love him. I am a better person because of him. He has been an absolute gift to my heart, and I can't imagine loving anyone the way I love him.

"It was the first time we said we love each other."

He smiles back at me. "And I haven't stopped falling in love with you since."

"Neither have I. Don't think I ever will either."

"Same," he says with a wink, and I squeeze his hand. "It was right around here," he says then, slowing down, and I keep my eyes peeled.

"I don't see it."

"I know it's here," he says quietly as he moves the phone with the flashlight around. I see something sparkle just as he says, "There it is!"

And sure as shit, a huge footprint is before us. "What the hell! Did you guys do this? Are you pranking me!" I accuse him, but he looks so serious. I look back, and once more, something sparkly catches my eyes. "Is there something stuck in the snow?" I bend down and reach into the footprint for the glittering thing. When I realize what it is, I turn to show Evan, but everyone is standing around us with lit candles in their hands. That's when I see Evan, on one knee. With his face illuminated by the candles, I can see the most sincere and loving look on his sweet face.

Everything stops.

My heart.

My breath.

Any coherent thought.

Hell, I'm pretty sure the snow has stopped.

"I had dinner with Aviva and Nico and asked for their blessing to marry you. I promised that I would love you more than I ever dreamed I was capable of. That I would take care of your well-being and your mental health just as you have taken care of mine. I promised that you would never want for anything and that you would always know your worth."

Tears burn my eyes as I hold his gaze with mine. "Oh, Evan."

"That was over six months ago, and the reason I've waited is because I wanted to give them time to adjust and to see that my promise is real." My heart skips probably a billion beats as I get lost in his loving eyes. "In my darkest hour, when I thought love wasn't ever going to happen for me, you came along. You brought light into my life, Callie, and loved even the darkest parts of me. My love for you is bigger than any Bigfoot out there."

I choke on my laughter as I drown in his gaze. "I love you, Evan."

He reaches up, taking the ring from my fingers. I cover my mouth to keep in the sob as he says, "I don't want to make fun of Bigfooters with anyone but you."

My voice is shaky as I agree, "I don't either."

Evan's lips start to tremble as he swallows hard. "Will you marry me?"

I drop down to my knees in the snow and take his hands in mine. "Yes, Evan. Yes. A thousand, million, trillion times, yes."

His face lights up as he finds my hand and puts the ring on it. I don't even care what it looks like because that doesn't matter to me. All that matters to me is that this man loves me and I'm his light. Just as he is mine. Our lips meet, and I wrap my arms around his neck, holding him close. I hear everyone cheering for us, but all I feel, all I see, is Evan.

As our eyes sparkle with the promise of our future, he whispers, "Sorry I couldn't get Nico and Aviva here. I guess he wasn't ready to accept it was going to happen, but I couldn't wait any longer."

I shrug, too happy to be bothered. "You're all I need," I whisper, and his eyes darken as he moves in closer, his lips ever so close to mine. "He'll come around."

"And even if he doesn't, I'm not going anywhere."

"Neither am I."

Once more, our lips meet as the snow falls and the lights twinkle around us. I miss my family and I wish they were here, but the more I think about it, I have my family in my arms.

Evan Adler is all I need.

Stupid Christmas

Quinn

Evan kisses his new fiancée with such love, even I get a little teary-eyed. Though, if you ask my mom, I'm a lot like Evan. Sensitive. I don't agree. I think I'm more like Owen, commanding and badass, but my brother isn't crying. Instead, he holds his soon-to-be wife while smiling widely at our newly engaged brother. Shelli and Aiden cuddle their son, and Posey leans into Boon, with Zac between them, everyone so excited and happy for the new future addition to our family.

Everything has changed.

It came out of nowhere, too. I feel as if we were all a unit, then Shelli found Aiden, Posey found Boon, Owen found Angie, and now Evan has Callie. It all happened so damn fast, and while I'm happy for my siblings, I find myself a little bit jealous. Which is stupid since I have a lot going on. I'm starting my second semester of residency this winter, and it's not going to be easy. I am going into a tough specialization, where I'll work solely on athletes who need sports-related surgeries. Mainly hockey players since that's whom I've been raised to love and appreciate.

Yet, I want what everyone else in my family has. It's really not fair to be raised by two parents who love so hard, their love for each other spills over onto you. I've watched my parents go through tough times, and even the greatest of times, and still, they stand together. I watched my brother-in-law Boon cry over my sister when he thought she might die. He stood beside her and even changed all the ways he eats just for her. Aiden is Shelli's peace, her calm. Owen has never smiled the way he does when Angie is around, and then Callie, well, she saved my brother Evan completely. So, of course, how could I not want someone to do the same for me? Someone to be my constant peace and happiness. The missing piece of my life.

Crazy thing is, I've found her. I just gotta lock her down.

Emery Brooks stands beside me, her braid lying along her shoulders with a red beanie on her head. She has a thick scarf around her neck, and she's wearing a big, poofy jacket. She hates being cold. When we were in Boston, she always had her hands up under my shirt or in my coat to keep warm. I let her, too, because I love her touch. I love how her nose turns red and how rosy her cheeks get. I move closer to her, snaking my hand around her waist. She looks up at me and then around at our families. Since they're all looking at Evan and Callie, she moves into me, leaning on my chest. I prop my head on hers and sigh happily.

I fell in love with Emery a year ago.

I'd always loved her as a friend. But then we were around each other a lot more with Shelli marrying Aiden, and we fell into a best friend kind of friendship. We talked constantly, and I never thought anything sexual about us. She was a little sister, I guess, but then it all changed when she found out I was a virgin. I can still hear her cackling laughter and remember how stupid she made me feel.

But then she kissed me.

And everything changed.

It was as if I were seeing her in a new light. Her lips are danger-ous, and her smile makes me forget every rational thought in my head. I was hooked from that moment on. Problem is, Emery doesn't want to be tied down. She told me from the jump we were friends with benefits, and because I want her so badly, I agreed. Which was not a smart move, because instead of being just friends and reaping all the dirty benefits imaginable, I fell in love with her. I remember it like it was yesterday. We were at a Billie Eilish concert, and we were singing "Ocean Eyes" loudly and obnox-iously. She looked at me, laughing, and I was a goner.

I am hers. Wholeheartedly.

I still don't know if she feels the same, but there is no stopping my feelings for her. When she told me not to fall for her, I ignored her, laughed it off, and continued to feel so deeply for her. Even after I walked into her family's restaurant and found her with another guy, I still love her. We got into a huge screaming match, and that's when I dumbly told her I loved her. Man, she was so pissed, and I was too. I think we both said things we regretted, but then I admitted that I loved her.

And she ghosted me.

Completely.

This is the first time I've seen her since that stupid moment in Brooks House. I didn't expect what happened in her room to happen, but now that it has, I feel like there is a chance. Surely she loves me. I swear she has to, because of the way she touched me, kissed me, held me, and how her eyes locked with mine. Or am I a love-sick fool?

When everyone starts for the happy couple, Emery quickly moves away from me, and I watch as she walks away without even looking back at me. Fuck me. I know I should congratulate my brother, but instead, I head inside. I kick off my boots and take off my winter gear before heading to the kitchen where my aunt Grace is sitting. She looks at me, and I look at her, both of us confused.

"You didn't go watch?"

She shakes her head. "Nope, watching the baby," she says, hooking her finger behind her. I look to where Alexis is fast asleep in her car seat. "Why aren't you out there?"

I shrug, walking over to the island counter and reaching for the bottle of Jack that's sitting in front of her. She doesn't stop me, nor does she question me as I pour a shot and down it quickly. I make a face at the fiery liquid before shaking my head. I'm not a drinker, but since I've seen other people do it and it seems to help, figured I'd try the same. When the liquid hits my gut, I find it doesn't help at all. I'm still thinking of Emery.

"Stupid Christmas."

Grace snorts. "Same, nephew. Same," she says, holding her glass up to me. She takes a long sip and shakes her head. "I hate the holidays. They make me miss James so much."

Well, don't I feel like an asshole. I'm standing here love-sick over a girl, and my aunt is still in love with her husband who passed. How unfair is that? "I'm sorry, Auntie."

She waves me off. "He'd be so excited that Ryan is having a baby and that Amelia's family keeps growing. I'm excited, but I'm sad he's not here with me to experience it and feel the joy together."

I nod. "He is, Auntie. He's always with you."

She smiles, tapping the back of my hand. "I know, sweetheart. Thank you." She takes in a deep breath and then sighs. "Do you think I should start dating?"

I grin. "Only if you want to," I say softly. "Though, FYI, the dating world is trash."

She laughs, and I smile back at her. "Ain't that the damn truth," she agrees, shaking her head. "Is that why you're in here drinking?"

"Yeah," I admit. "Pretty sure I fell in love with the wrong girl."

"How so?"

"I don't think she wants a relationship with me."

"Oh, Quinny. You're so young. You can wait."

"I don't want to. I love her."

Her brow perks. "Emery?"

"That's her."

"Good girl, genius, beautiful," she says, and then she smiles. "Reminds me a lot of me."

"No way. You two are nothing alike. She's crazy."

"She's driven, smart, and knows what she wants. I am, same as when I was younger. That's why James loved me so. But I wouldn't settle. I wanted to see the world, have fun, not be tied down. But James was relentless. He wanted me and didn't stop until he had me." I can see the pain on my aunt's face, and I can feel it too. James was an incredible uncle and an even better father and husband. He loved with his whole being. "Have you told her how you feel?"

"Yeah, but it was shitty and in the middle of an argument. Though, I did tell her I loved her again this afternoon, and she said, 'I know.'" Grace grimaces, and I laugh. "Yeah. So there's that."

She leans in, and our eyes lock. "Can I give you some advice?"

I think that's my favorite thing about Grace. Unlike everyone else, she always asks if we want her advice. She doesn't give it unsolicited; she offers it. "Sure."

"One more time. Tell her how you feel, and tell her what you want. If she doesn't want to give it to you, then walk away. Sometimes you have to let go of someone, even when it feels like you're losing a limb. It may feel like she's the one for you, but you can't put your heart into someone who doesn't want you."

I nod. "It just sucks 'cause she's my best friend."

Grace's lips turn down as she gives me a gloomy look. "Oh, Quinny. I'm sorry."

"I don't know. Maybe you're right. One more time. See what happens, and then try to move on."

"Yeah, and you never know. Maybe she's not ready now, but in the future, she might be and y'all can reconnect."

"Are you saying to wait for her?"

"Absolutely not. I'm saying maybe right now isn't the time for you. Maybe you two have some growing to do, and then you'll meet back up."

Grace's thought process is terrifying because I want so badly for Emery to be mine. I don't know if I can move on, or if I even want to. I love how we are together. I love how it feels to be around her, and most of all, I love laughing with her. What if the only reason it's like that is because I haven't been with anyone else?

Why is this so hard? Was it hard for everyone else like this?

"Did you and James meet back up?"

She smiles, her cheeks filling with color. "I was burned a lot before meeting him, and I broke up with him when he told me he loved me."

"Ha, maybe you two are the same. That's how it went down."

"But then I found out I was pregnant, and from that moment on, James and I didn't part. But I don't suggest that."

I laugh. "I'm not knocking anyone up, Auntie. I just want her to love me."

Grace reaches out and cups my face. "Baby, you are worthy of love. And if she doesn't want to give it to you, then maybe she's not as smart as she seems. Remember that, though, and don't settle for anything but greatness."

I bite the inside of my lip, but before I can say anything else, everyone starts to file in. They're all so loud, so happy and excited, it makes me sick. I move around the island and hug my aunt from behind. She kisses my wrist and then taps my face before I go into the great room. A huge table is still full of all the platters of food we had for dinner. While everyone comes back in and warms up, I snack on some green beans before I notice the piano.

While we are a hockey-playing family, we are also a musical family. Usually we have a script at the holidays with all our parts for the caroling, but Mom figured this year, with everyone being here, we wouldn't have time. I pop a green bean into my mouth and head to the piano, sitting on the bench. I make sure it's tuned before I start to play "Silent Night." I'm not much of a singer, but I can carry a tune. I move my fingers along the keys, playing effortlessly and singing the way I would when I was younger. When Shelli pops her head in, hitting a note only she can, I smile. She leans on the piano, singing with me, and then Mom joins. I love singing with my mom and sister. They have such beautiful ranges and are two gorgeous singers.

Evan comes in, sitting beside me as I start "O Come, All Ye Faithful." Soon, the whole room is singing, and I notice that everyone has come into the great room. Some sitting on the floor, some at the table, but it's Emery I notice standing in the doorway.

Her sweet eyes are on me.

I swallow hard as my dad comes to sit on the other side of me, on the edge of a chair, playing a guitar. I wish I could get lost in being with my family, singing with them as we would growing up, but my eyes keep cutting to Emery's. She looks so unsure of herself, which makes no sense to me. Doesn't she realize she can walk into any room and take it over? She's so witty, so fucking beautiful, and I can't get enough of her. She's wearing a rather large Assassins team sweatshirt and tight leggings with fuzzy socks. Her hair is in a tight braid, and her lashes kiss her cheeks every time she blinks. Her lips are so thick, and fuck, I just want her.

As the song ends, Posey says, "See, Mom, you can't get mad if you aren't going to make everyone a script of what part to sing."

Mom glares. "I'm giving signs and pointing!"

"You're not a conductor," Shelli says, and Mom scoffs.

"Shelli Grace, I am the conductor of this family."

Everyone laughs at that. Well, everyone but me. Instead, I start to play the notes to "Ocean Eyes," and I'm not sure why. I don't know if it's because she's looking at me or if I was just thinking about it, but I can't stop myself. My fingers move over the keys, and of course, I get some very odd looks. Evan has my back, though. He sings softly along with me, and when I get to the chorus, I look up to meet Emery's eyes. As I sing, her eyes don't leave mine, and I know everyone is watching and is confused. Some may know we have something, but no one knows the extent of it. Not even our moms.

When Mom starts to knock on the piano, we look up at her as we stop playing. She gives me a sweet look. "Honey, it's Christmas Eve, not Billie Eve."

The room fills with laughter, but I notice Emery has walked out of the room. I get up, almost knocking Dad off.

"Damn, Quinn!"

"My bad, Dad," I say, patting his back and then rushing after Emery. I don't find her in the living room or even the kitchen. I check her room, but she's not there. Out the window, I spot her on the enclosed deck. I head back to the great room where our families are still singing loudly and then through the living room to the deck. Emery doesn't even glance back at me. She stands with a blanket wrapped around her, staring out at the darkness. I'm unsure of what she is looking at since it's just black out there. There aren't even stars in the sky, and the moon has been covered by clouds.

I clear my throat. "Looking for Santa?" She doesn't laugh, and when I see a tear trickle down her cheek, I quickly wipe it away. "Don't cry."

"Quinn, I don't want to hurt you."

But those words hurt just the same. "Oh."

Silence moves between us, and I don't even hear our families anymore; I'm too engrossed in her. Emery brings her hand up, moving it along her other cheek, and then she shakes her head. "I don't want to lose your friendship, but I can't do this."

I swallow hard, my heart almost beating out of my chest. "Why? We're great together, Em. I love you."

She closes her eyes. "I know. But don't you see?" she asks,

looking up at me. "I could fall fully in love with you, and I'd be married and pregnant within a year. I don't want that. I have so much to do. I have so many things I want to experience. And travel. I want to travel, but—"

"Why can't we do all that together? I want to be there, to support you, and to love you through everything. No one says we have to be married or pregnant. That's insane! We have all the time in the world for that."

"But if I allowed myself to love you, I'd end up like that." Her eyes burn into mine. "I would become so engrossed in you that my dreams, my aspirations, wouldn't matter."

"No, that's fucking stupid. We can have our own dreams and support each other. Look at our parents. If they can do it, we can."

But she just shakes her head. "I can't. Call me selfish, but I know how I am. I know how I'd love you, and it's not fair to me."

"I'd love you the same, though. I don't understand."

"Quinn, we haven't experienced anything! You haven't slept with anyone but me or had your heart broken. I haven't even had my heart broken yet—"

"So, you're fine breaking mine?" I ask, holding her gaze.

"I think if we stop this now, walk away from each other, we can do it cleanly."

I laugh without humor. "There is nothing clean about this. I love you, Em. I love you despite the fact that I'm pretty sure you could kill me and hide the body and get away with it."

I say it to make her smile, but she doesn't. Instead, her tears fall faster. "Quinn."

"Let's try, see how it goes. I promise I won't ask you to marry me for five years."

But she shakes her head again. "I can't love you right now."

I feel my eyes burning. "Right now? So, what? You want me to wait?"

"No. I would never ask that," she insists, holding my gaze. "I'm sure there is someone out there who will love you more and be everything you think I am."

"Absolutely not. There is no one like you. No one who makes me feel like you do."

"Because you haven't met her," she asserts. "A girl out there who's ready to be like our siblings and parents. But that's not me. I have too much going on, and so do you. But after this afternoon, hearing you say those words, I know we can't keep things simple between us. There is too much here, and it scares me. I feel tied down by it, and I don't like that feeling."

A sob burns my throat as I hold her gaze. "So, you don't love me?"

She swallows hard, looking away. "Please don't make me answer that."

"I think I deserve the answer."

"Maybe. But I don't want to hurt you or make you think there is a chance things could change."

I hate it when a tear slides down my face. But maybe Mom is right and I am sensitive. I reach out, pulling Emery into my arms, and she comes without hesitation. Our lips meet almost instantly, and I kiss her like it could be the last time I ever feel her lips against mine. I tangle my fingers in her hair, and I hold her tighter than I mean to. But I have to. When we part, we're both breathless and gasping for air.

"Just tell me to wait for you," I whisper as I slide my nose along hers.

She strokes her fingers over my cheek as she hiccups a sob. "I can't. I wouldn't do that to you."

"I would, though."

"I know, which is why I won't ask."

I squeeze my eyes shut tighter and press my nose into hers. "I love you, Emery, and I think I always will."

She touches her lips to mine instead of answering, and I think that hurts me even more. I pull away first and then back away, wiping my face and mouth. When I open my eyes, she has covered her mouth, her eyes glossy and so full of sorrow. I want to hate her, I want to be so mad that she has broken me, but I can't. I get where she is coming from. Seeing our parents and siblings so in love and how they have all become one, I get it. She doesn't want to lose her identity, who she is, but I wish she could realize I wouldn't want that for her. That we can be two people in love and still stay individuals. Or maybe we can't. I don't know. Maybe we are too young.

With a shaky voice, I say, "Merry Christmas, Emery."

Her eyes gut me, they are so sad, but still, she whispers, "Merry Christmas, Quinny."

Unable to stand there any longer, I turn and leave, thinking there is nothing merry about this Christmas—or any to come.

Because Emery isn't mine.

THE END

Acknowledgments

Life has not been kind to me. This is my tenth birthday/holiday without my mom, and I feel like her passing just happened yesterday. I lost my job with my kids because the director didn't like me, and I just don't understand that. How do you uproot children's lives like that? But I rose above, and I continue to do so. My depression has been the worst ever, but thankfully, I am managing it. I'm not suicidal, which is a blessing in itself. I'm just over crying, and I feel like this book was a gift to me. It brought me back into a world where happiness and love are key. While there was some sadness in my Assassins world, I feel like it's a part of life. As Mark Frost said, there is no light without darkness.

Lisa, Franci, and Rue, thank you for always being the best team a girl could get. I love you. Merry Christmas.

To my friends and family, I wouldn't be who I am without you, and I love all of you.

I love you, Michael, Mikey, Alyssa, and Phoebe.

And to you, thank you for always standing beside me, supporting me, and cheering me on.

I am beyond grateful for you.

Thank you.

Love,
    Toni

Also by Toni Aleo

Clipped by Love

Hooked by Love

End Game

Spiked by Love

Saved by Love

IceCats Series

Juicy Rebound

Wild Tendy

Hard Hit

All the Sauce

Taking Risks

Whiskey Prince

Becoming the Whiskey Princess

Whiskey Rebellion

Patchwork Series

(Paranormal)

Pieces

Broken Pieces

Spring Grove Novels

(Small-town romances)

Not the One

Small-Town Sweetheart

Standalones

Let it be Me

Two-Man Advantage

Misadventures

(Standalones)

Misadventures with a Rookie

Misadventures of a Manny

Assassins Series

Taking Shots

Trying to Score

Empty Net

Falling for the Backup

Blue Lines

About Toni Aleo

WALL STREET JOURNAL, NEW YORK TIMES AND USA TODAY BEST SELLING AUTHOR TONI ALEO IS AN AUTHOR YOU CAN'T MISS!

make sure to Join my Mailing List: https://www.subscribepage.com/tonialeonewsletter

My name is Toni aleo and I'm a #PredHead, #sherrio, #potterhead, and part of the #familybusiness!

I am also a wife to my amazing husband, mother of a future airman and a gymnast, and also a fur momma to Phoebe, Gaston el Papillon & Winston.

You can usually find me hollering for the whole Nashville Predators since I'll never give my heart to one player again. When I'm not in the gym getting swole, I'm usually writing, trying to make my dreams a reality or being a taxi for my kids. I'm obsessed with Harry Potter, Supernatural, Disney and anything that sparkles! I'm pretty sure I was Belle in a past life and if I could be on any show it would be supernatural so I can hunt with Sam and Dean.

Also, could I LOVE hockey anymore?

www.tonialeo.com
toni@tonialeo.com

Printed in Great Britain
by Amazon